THREE FLUTE F...

1
PAVANE

FLUTE

MICHAEL JACQUES

AB 2185

2
AYRE

IV

RIGAUDON

Processed and printed by
Halstan & Co. Ltd., Amersham, Bucks., England

THREE FLUTE FANCIES

1
PAVANE

MICHAEL JACQUES

2
AYRE

3
RIGAUDON

8

Dal Segno al 🔶
e poi la Coda

CODA

Processed and printed by
Halstan & Co. Ltd., Amersham, Bucks., England